DC SUPER HERO GIRLS™

PAST TIMES AT SUPER HERO HIGH

a graphic novel

WRITTEN BY
Shea Fontana

ART BY
Yancey Labat, Agnes Garbowska, and **Marcelo DiChiara**

ADDITIONAL BREAKDOWNS BY
Carl Potts

COLORS BY
Monica Kubina, Silvana Brys, and **Jeremy Lawson**

LETTERING BY
Janice Chiang

DC SUPER HERO GIRLS: PAST TIMES AT SUPER HERO HIGH. Published by DC Comics, 2900 W. Alameda Avenue, Burbank, CA 91505. GST # is R125921072. This book is manufactured at a facility holding chain-of-custody certification. This paper is made with sustainably managed North American fiber. For Advertising and Custom Publishing contact dccomicsadvertising@dccomics.com. For details on DC Comics Ratings, visit dccomics.com/go/ratings. Printed by Transcontinental Interglobe, Beauceville, QC, Canada. 12/14/17. Second Printing. ISBN: 978-1-4012-7383-5

PEFC Certified
Printed on paper from sustainably managed forests and controlled sources
www.pefc.org
PEFC
PEFC/01-31-106

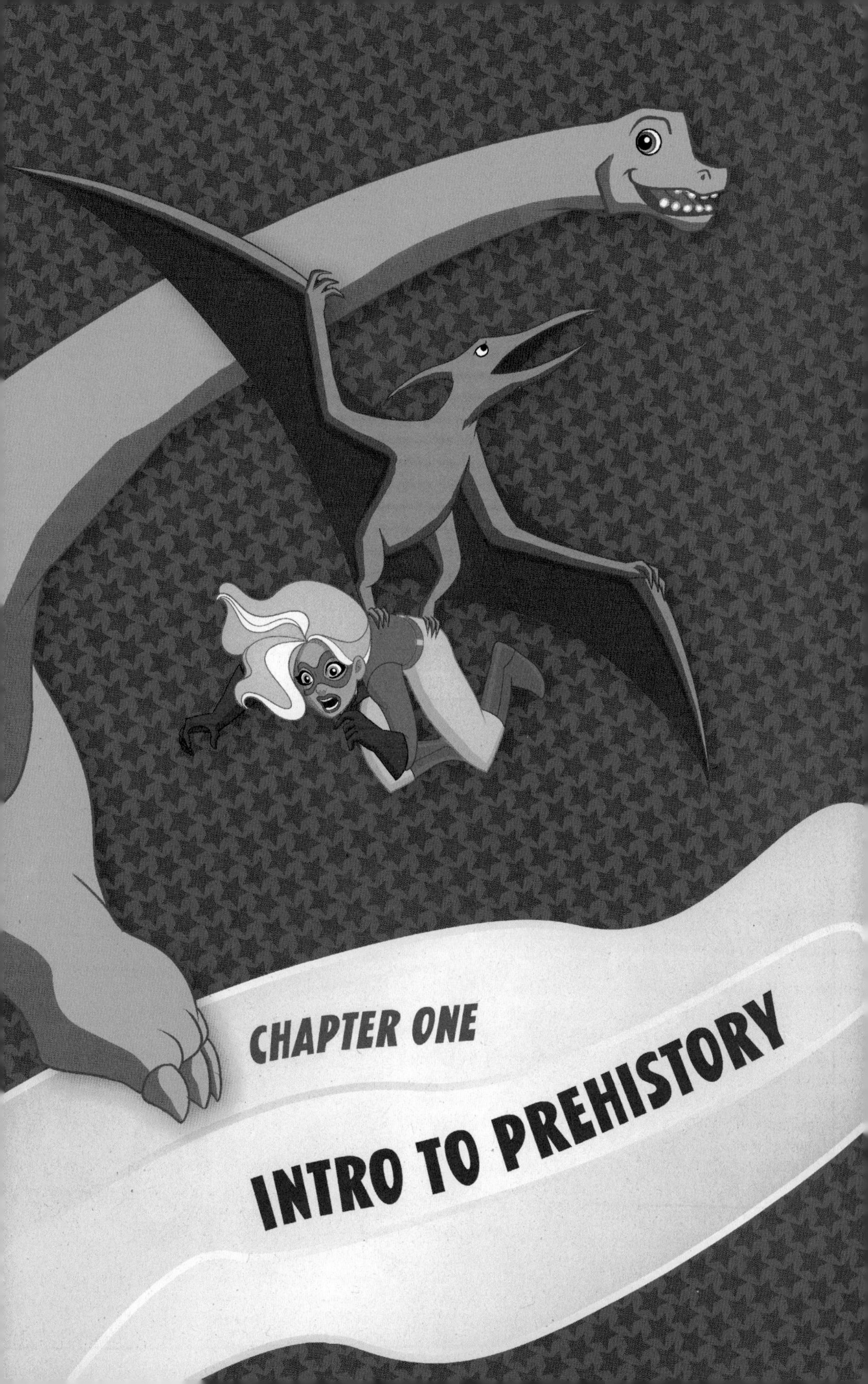

CHAPTER ONE

INTRO TO PREHISTORY

ZZZZZZIP!
POW!
TKK!
WHOOSH
KLUNK!
SCHOOL BUS
FIELD TRIP ON!

MORNING, SUPERGIRL!
HAND ME YOUR PERMISSION SLIPS AS YOU BOARD THE TIME MACHINE!
HERE YOU GO, MISS LIBERTY BELLE.
WOW, BATGIRL. YOU'RE REALLY INTO THIS DINOSAUR FIELD TRIP, HUH?
I LIKE DINOS SO MUCH I'M MAKING A GIANT MECHANICAL ONE FOR MY BAT-BUNKER! BASICALLY, I'M THEIR BIGGEST FAN!
I ♥ DINOSAURS
I HOPE YOU FIND THE FIELD TRIP BOTH EXCITING AND EDUCATIONAL!
I'VE ALREADY READ EVERYTHING ON DINOSAURS! I CAN'T WAIT TO GET UP CLOSE AND PERSONAL SO I CAN LEARN SOMETHING NEW.
WAIT FOR ME!

HOLD THE BUS!
I grant permission for my student Harley Quinn to attend Miss Liberty Belle's prehistory field trip. Signed, Harley's Mom
UNH!
TRIP!
YIKES!
CRASH!
GOLLY GEE, HARLEY!
OOPSIE-POOPSIES! LET ME GET THOSE FOR YA!
I grant permission for my student Wonder Woman to attend Miss Liberty Belle's prehistory field trip. Signed, Hippolyta
EVERYTHING'S IN ORDER HERE, MISS B!

HEYA, FELLOW FIELDTRIPPERS!
-NGH!- HARLEY!
YA SAVED THE FRONT SEAT FOR ME!
BATS, AREN'T YA JUST BURSTIN' WITH EXCITEMENT TO SEE SOME DINOS?
I CAN'T WAIT!
LET ME KNOW IF YA HAVE ANY QUESTIONS!
NOBODY KNOWS MORE ABOUT DINOS THAN YOURS TRULY, THE NUMBER ONE TOP BANANA OF DINOSAUR FANS--ME!
WE'LL SEE ABOUT THAT.
YOU'RE NOT JOINING US ON THE FIELD TRIP, BUMBLEBEE? IT'S SURE TO BE THE BEE'S KNEES!
THIS BEE'S TUMMY DISAGREES. JUST THINKING OF TIME TRAVEL MAKES ME MOTION SICK!
I'LL STAY HERE AND DO THE DINOSAUR BOOK REPORT INSTEAD.

THE PAST IS DANGEROUS. RULE NUMBER ONE IS NO ONE LEAVES THE BUS. PERIOD.
YOU GOTS IT, MAMA! I'M NOT GOIN' ANYWHERES!
NON-INTERFERENCE SHIELD
AS LONG AS WE REMAIN IN THE BUS, WE ARE PROTECTED AGAINST INTERFERING WITH THE PAST AND CHANGING THE FUTURE.
PAST
145,000,000 YEARS
HOLD ON TO YOUR CAPES!
WE'RE GOING JURASSIC!
HAVE A GOOD, ER, PAST!
SUPER HERO HIGH
WHOA!
SUPER HERO HIGH

1900
1800
1700
SCHOOL BUS
1400
1300
10,000 B.C.
70,000 B.C.
OH MY GOOSE GRASS!
I SPY WITH MY LITTLE EYE SOMETHING THAT IS RED.
SUPERGIRL! YOU'RE NOT SUPPOSED TO USE YOUR X-RAY VISION DURING I SPY!
WHAT ARE YOU DOING, BEAST BOY?
Y'SEE, KATANA, IF YOU HOLD YOUR BREATH THE WHOLE TIME YOU'RE TIME TRAVELIN', IT'S GOOD LUCK.
AW MAN! MMF!
HA! MADE YA BREATHE!

DID YOU KNOW THAT "DINOSAUR" IS GREEK FOR "TERRIBLE LIZARD"?
OF COURSE I DID. PALEONTOLOGY WAS MY FIRST FORAY INTO DETECTIVE WORK.
I WAS FOLLOWING IN THE STEPS OF MARY ANNING--IF YOU KNOW WHO THAT IS.
MARY ANNING. FOUND THE FIRST ICHTHYOSAUR, AMONG OTHER MAJOR DISCOVERIES. AND MY PERSONAL HERO!
I BETCHA I KNOW MORE ABOUT DINOS THAN YOU!
NO WAY! WHEN WE GET THERE, I'LL PROVE THAT I KNOW THE MOST!
YOU BOTH KNOW MORE ABOUT DINOSAURS THAN ME!
THEMYSCIRA ELEMENTARY WASN'T BIG ON NATURAL HISTORY.
HOT SOCKS! WE'RE HERE, KIDDOS!

OH MY--
STEGOSAURUS!
CRUNCH
DO YOU KNOW WHAT THAT BIG ONE IS?
DIPLODOCUS!
NO FAIR! I COULDN'T SEE PAST YOUR NOGGIN!

OOH, OOH! I SPY A WHOLE PACK OF T. REX.
ACTUALLY, THOSE ARE ALLOSAURUSES.
CONTRARY TO IDEAS PERPETUATED BY MAJOR MOTION PICTURES, TYRANNOSAURUS REX DIDN'T EXIST DURING THE JURASSIC ERA.
WHATEVER THEY ARE, THEY'RE HEADED RIGHT FOR US!
GREAT GARDENIAS!
ÜBER SHARP TEETH!

GRRR!
SNIKT!
ROOOOOOO
OOAR!
AAAAAAGH!
SCHOOL BUS

WHATEVER IT IS, IT HAS BIG, POINTY TEETH AND A HANKERING FOR SUPER HERO SANDWICH!
BEAT IT, YOU BRUTE!
KRRRRK!
THIS NEWFANGLED BUS DOESN'T HANDLE ANYTHING LIKE MY OL' MODEL T. THAT CAR COULD 23 SKIDOO!
I CAN DRIVE! I ACED MY ***EVASIVE MANEUVERING*** TEST!
HAVE AT IT, DOLL!
WHY DOES BATS GET TO DRIVE? I LIKE DRIVIN'!

SKREEEEEEEE!
VRRROOOM!
YEAH! SAVED BY THE BAT!
WOOO!
LUCKILY, DINOSAURS ARE EASY TO ESCAPE BECAUSE THEY HAVE RELATIVELY SMALL BRAINS.

BLINK!

I THINK THE PEANUT BRAIN BEHIND YA WOULD DISAGREE!

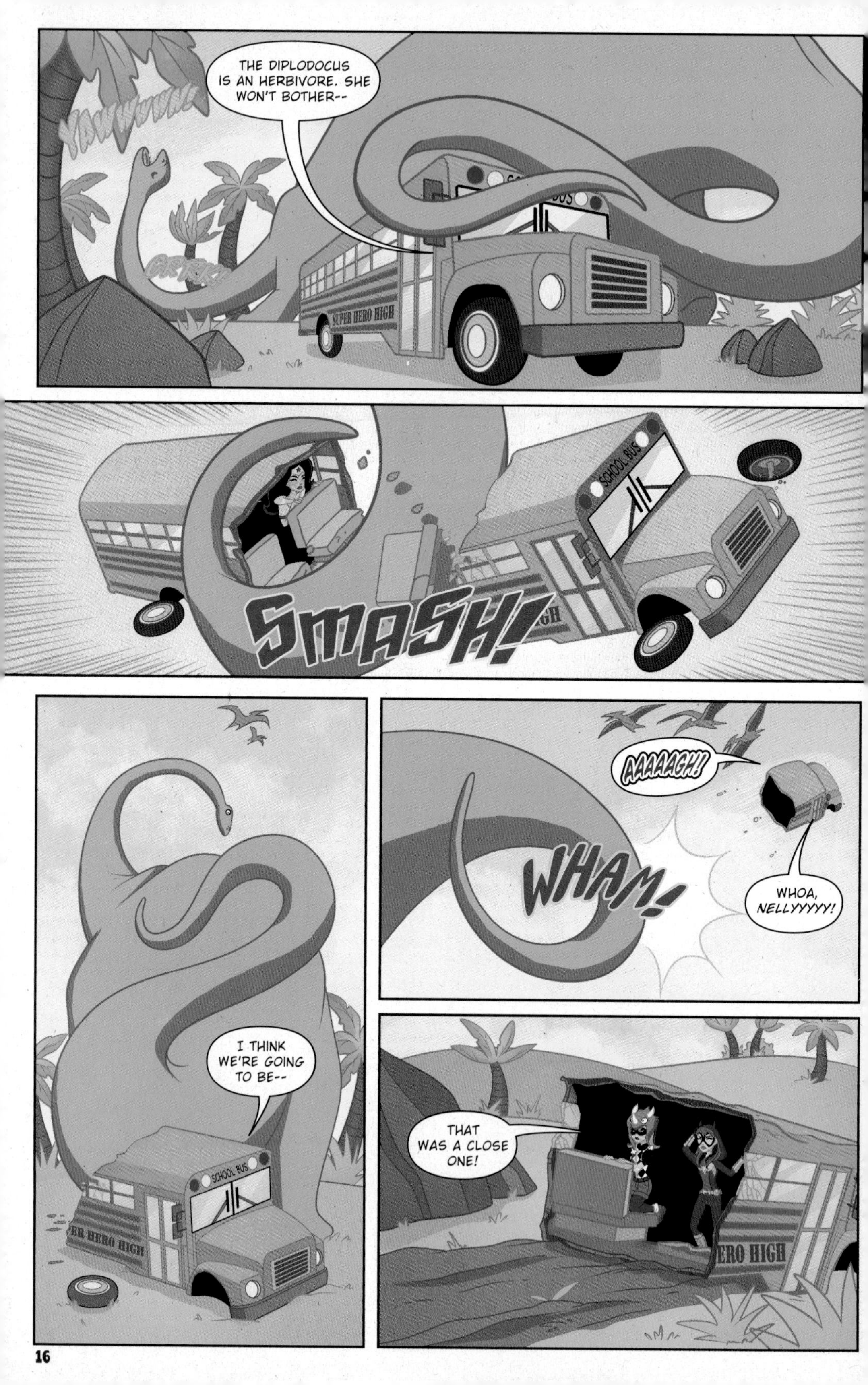
THE DIPLODOCUS IS AN HERBIVORE. SHE WON'T BOTHER--
YAWWWWN!
GRRRR!
SUPER HERO HIGH
SCHOOL BUS
SMASH!
AAAAAGH!
WHAM!
WHOA, NELLYYYYY!
I THINK WE'RE GOING TO BE--
SCHOOL BUS
ER HERO HIGH
THAT WAS A CLOSE ONE!
ERO HIGH

EVERYBODY STAY INSIDE!
MISS BELLE SAID AS LONG AS WE'RE IN THE BUS, WE CAN'T DO ANYTHING TO MESS UP THE FUTURE.
TIME TRAVEL RULES
1. STAY INSIDE OF THE BUS.
2. TAKE NOTHING, LEAVE NOTHING.
3. ALERT DRIVER IF YOU SUSPECT ALTERATION OF TIME.
I KNEW YOU SHOULD NEVER TRUST AN HERBIVORE! NASTY PLANT-EATER!
WHOA, IVY! DON'T GO STEREOTYPIN' US VEGETARIANS. WE DIDN'T ALL THROW MISS BELLE, BATGIRL, AND HARLEY ACROSS THE JUNGLE!
THE FRONT OF THE BUS COULDN'T HAVE GONE VERY FAR.
KATANA'S RIGHT. THEY'LL BE HERE SOON!
SOUNDS LIKE I GOTS TIME FOR A CAT NAP!

MISS BELLE MUST'VE BEEN STUCK IN THE BACK OF THE BUS WHEN WE WENT FLYING. SHE'LL BE HERE FOR US ASAP!
DOUBTFUL!
WHY DO YOU HAVE TO ARGUE WITH EVERYTHING I SAY?
I DON'T HAFTA. I REALLY THOUGHT IT WAS DOUBTFUL SINCE MISS BELLE IS CURRENTLY BEING TEACHER-NAPPED BY A PTERODACTYL.

AW, APPLESAUCE! THIS BRUTE'S GOT ME BY THE BRITCHES!
WE HAVE TO SAVE HER!
MMM-HMM.
YOU NEED TO TAKE THIS SERIOUSLY! MISS BELLE IS THE ONLY ONE WHO KNOWS HOW TO OPERATE THE TIME MACHINE.
I KNOW, BATTY-PANTS. YA DON'T HAVE TO BURST MY BUBBLE!
POP!

EXIT
EMERGENCY EXIT ONLY
GROWLL!
MISS BELLE BETTER GET HERE ON THE DOUBLE CUZ I AM STARVIN'!
SNIFF! SNIFF!
GROWLL!
ALLS I HAD FOR BREAKFAST WAS THREE WAFFLES, SIX BANANAS, FOUR BOWLS OF QUACKOPUFFS, TWO SLICES OF LEFTOVER PIZZA...
SLURP!
...AND HALF OF AN ENGLISH MUFFIN--I'M WATCHIN' MY FIGURE.
BEAST BOY ISN'T THE ONLY ONE HUNGRY FOR LUNCH. STAND ASIDE, LIZARD-LIPS!

GRRRR!
EXIT
EMERGENCY EXIT ONLY
I MEANT "LIZARD-LIPS" AS A COMPLIMENT!
WE HAVE TO BREAK THE RULES BEFORE THAT DINO BREAKS US!
LET'S GET OUT OF HERE!
THIS QUALIFIES AS AN EMERGENCY!
HANG ON!
I GOT YOU, BEAST BOY!
THIS IS THE CLOSEST I'VE EVER BEEN TO A GIRL HOLDIN' MY HAND!
-NGN!-
CHOMP!

REMEMBER WHAT MISS BELLE ALWAYS SAID IN PREHISTORY PREP?
"STOP PASSING NOTES, SUPERGIRL"?
NO, THE OTHER THING SHE ALWAYS SAID. "IF YOU GET LOST IN THE PAST, DON'T DISTURB ANYTHING."
KRUNCH!
KLAK!
KRUNCH!
SHH! IF WE DON'T WANT TO DISTURB ANYTHING, WE NEED TO BE STEALTHY. BLEND IN.
I GOTS IT, MAMA!
I CALL IT THE BRACHIO-BLEND-IN-OSAURUS!

UH-OH. WE GOT COMPANY.
WHAT UP, BRACHIO-BROS?
GRRRRR!
I THINK THEY LIKE YOU, BEAST BOY!
BUT I THINK THAT ONE DOESN'T LIKE YOU.
ROOOAR!

CHAPTER TWO
THE DINO EGG EFFECT

WANNA PLAY TEETH VERSUS SWORDS, BIG BOY?
NO, KATANA! IF WE FIGHT IT, WE'RE INTERFERING WITH THE FUTURE!
-NGH!- LIKE LOSING OUR FRIENDS AND TEACHER IN THE JURASSIC ERA ISN'T INTERFERING?
DON'T WORRY, MAMAS! I GOTS THIS!
CHOMP!
JUST NEED TO LEVEL WITH HIM, STEGOSAURUS TO STEGOSAURUS.
GRRR?
RAWR, RAWR, DINO-DUDE!
OH MY HOLLYHOCKS!
BEAST BOY'S THE ALPHA DINO?!

SOON...
FRIENDS, DINOS, COUNTRY-REPTILIANS, LEND ME THE NERVE CANALS IN YOUR SKULL THAT ARE USED FOR HEARING!
I NEVER THOUGHT I'D SEE ANYTHING LIKE THIS, WONDER WOMAN!
HERBIVORES HANGING OUT WITH CARNIVORES?
NO, BEAST BOY BEING SO ELOQUENT!
LET US NOT EAT ONE ANOTHER, BUT INSTEAD LOVE OUR FELLOW DINOSAURS!

THE DAMAGE IS MOSTLY COSMETIC. I CAN GET THIS BABY UP AND RUNNING IN A FLASH!
OF COURSE YA CAN, BATS. YOU KNOW HOW TO DO EVERYTHING.
THEN, WE'LL BE ON OUR WAY TO RESCUE MISS LIBERTY BELLE FROM THAT PTERODACTYL IN NO TIME!
HERO HIGH
ANYTHING I CAN DO TO HELP GET THIS SHOW ON THE ROAD?
NOPE. I HAVE IT UNDER CONTROL, HARLEY.
CLANK!
CLINK!
CLANK!
ER HERO HIGH
SIGH.

POW! TIME MACHINE ON!
VRRROOMM!
VVVVVVRMMMM
PER HERO HIGH
LUCKILY, I KEEP A PAIR OF BINOCULARS IN MY BACKPACK! PERFECT FOR SPOTTIN' LOST TEACHERS!
I FOUND A CLUE!
OF COURSE YA DID.
HELP!
MISS BELLE!

AS A SEMIPROFESSIONAL NOVICE TREE-CLIMBER, I SAY WE COULD CREATE A SERIES OF FOOTHOLDS IN THE BARK AND--
DON'T WORRY! I GOT US COVERED.
TKK!
OF COURSE YA DO.
I KNEW MY CRACKERJACK KIDS WOULD COME FOR ME! THANK YOU, DOLLS!
DON'T THANK ME. BATGIRL DID ALL THE HEAVY LIFTIN'.

SLNK!
WE BETTER GET YOU OUT OF HERE BEFORE MAMA PTERODACTYL COMES HOME FOR DINNER.
COME ON, HARLEY!
RIGHT BEHIND YA!
IF I HAD MY OWN PET PTERODACTYL, NO WAY BATS COULD TOP ME THEN!
WELCOME TO THE QUINN FAMILY!

YEAH, BABY! HARLEY QUINN STICKS THE LANDING. A PERFECT TEN!
HURRY UP, HARLEY!
I DON'T EVEN GET ONE MOMENT TO RELISH MY SPECTACULAR, DEATH-DEFYIN', AWARD-WORTHY PERFORMANCE?
?
SKREEEEEE!
SKREEEEEEEEEE!

NOM-NOM-NOM!
DO YOU HAVE TO EAT RARE PREHISTORIC PLANTS RIGHT IN FRONT OF ME?!
I'M HUNGRY AND BEAST BOY WON'T LET ME EAT ANY DINOS.
NOT EVEN A LITTLE ONE.
TREAT YOUR FELLOW DINOS AS YOU WOULD LIKE TO BE TREATED AND--
I KNEW MISS BELLE WOULD BE BACK FOR US!
VVRRROOM!
SCHOOL BUS

EVERYBODY INTO THE TIME MACHINE!
SUPER HER
SKKKKKK!
AW, MAN! I WAS GETTIN' USED TO BEING THEIR POWERFUL BUT BENEVOLENT LEADER!
THANK HERA! I DIDN'T WANT TO LIVE IN A WORLD WITHOUT MODERN PLUMBING.
OR TEXT MESSAGES!
EXCUSE ME. IF YOU WOULDN'T MIND SQUEEZING IN A LITTLE?
PUBLIC TRANSPORTATION CAN BE SO CROWDED.

EVEN THOUGH I GOTTA GO, I GOT MY WAYS OF KNOWIN' WHAT HAPPENS, AND I WAS SERIOUS ABOUT THAT NOT EATING EACH OTHER THING!
BEAST BOY, NOW!
WHAT'S THE RUSH, MAMA? I THOUGHT WE HAD TIME TO KILL!
NOT IF TIME KILLS US FIRST!
SKREEE! SKREEEE! SKREEE!
WHOA! WHO INVITED THE PTERODACTYLS?
SCHOOL BUS
SUPER H

ZZZZZOOOOOM!
WAIT FOR ME!
SCHOOL BUS
CLICK!
PAST FUTURE
JUST A BIT MORE JUICE AND WE'LL BE READY TO BLOW THIS JOINT!
PHEW!
YIIIII!
READY FOR TIME TRAVEL!
START
FULL
HELP!
SKREEEEE!

STAY AWAY FROM MY IVY!
SKRF
THANKS!
WE'RE NOT OUTTA DODGE YET. MISTAH CRANKY BEAK HAS PALS IN HIGH PLACES!
FANCY SEEIN' YOU GALS HERE!
NO HERO LEFT BEHIND.
ESPECIALLY NOT MILLIONS OF YEARS BEHIND!
ANYBODY TAKE COACH WILDCAT'S DINOSAUR COMBAT ELECTIVE?
NEGATIVE.
I DID BASKET WEAVING INSTEAD.
NUH-UH.
THEN WE JUST WING IT!

DINO-FIGHT!
DID I SAY YOU SHOULDN'T FIGHT EACH OTHER?
I MEANT...
...YOU SHOULD ONLY FIGHT EACH OTHER WHEN YOUR BRILLIANT AND HANDSOME LEADER IS BEING ATTACKED.
WHOA. WITH GREAT POWER COMES...
...GREAT ABILITY TO INSTIGATE AWESOMENESS! WOOT-WOOT!

-EW!- DINO BREATH!
HSSSSSS!
NOW THAT TREE'S A HUGGER!
BONK
HERE'S A LESSON FROM THE FUTURE: DON'T TRY TO SNEAK UP ON A NINJA.
HEYA, BIRD BRAIN! YOU'RE GONNA BE EXTINCT. YOU WON'T EVEN MAKE IT THROUGH A LITTLE ICE AGE!
WHAT ARE YOU DOING?
USIN' PSYCHOLOGICAL MANIPULATION TO MESS WITH THEIR SELF-ESTEEM!

BAM!
HURRY, KIDS!
ROOOAR!
C'MON! LET'S GET OUT OF HERE!
OKAY, MISS BELLE! GET US BACK TO OUR FUTURE!

100,000,000
47,000,000
600
0
WHAT A HUMDINGER OF A FIELD TRIP!
I HAVEN'T HAD SO MUCH FUN SINCE COOLIDGE WAS IN OFFICE!
BUT, MISS BELLE, DIDN'T WE POTENTIALLY ALTER THE COURSE OF HISTORY WITH OUR ACTIONS?
THAT LITTLE SKIRMISH? NAH! OUR PREHISTORIC PALS WERE FIGHTING EACH OTHER LONG BEFORE WE ARRIVED.
AS LONG AS NOBODY DID ANYTHING RECKLESS, EVERYTHING WILL BE JUST DUCKY!

PLUNK!
HERO HIGH
OH SWEET LUCKY LINDBERGH! SUPER HERO HIGH IS STILL HERE!
I THOUGHT YOU KNEW WE WERE GOING TO BE "DUCKY."
TIME TRAVELING'S TRICKY BUSINESS. BEST NOT TO PUT OUT NEGATIVE VIBES WHEN YOU'RE IN THE TIME VORTEX!
I BETTER GET TO IT. A MESS LIKE THAT MEANS I'LL HAVE TO FILL OUT AN INCIDENT REPORT FOR PRINCIPAL WALLER.
ALL'S WELL THAT ENDS WELL, RIGHT, BATS?
YEP.
I THOUGHT FOR SURE SOMETHING WE DID IN THE PAST WOULD MAKE MODERN HUMANS HAVE LIZARD TONGUES, OR A THIRD EYE--
OR WEBBED TOES!
WAIT, YOU GUYS DON'T ALREADY HAVE THOSE?
HAHA HAHA HA HA!

NO LAUGHING! YOU KNOW THE RULES!
YEAH, I KNOW ALL THE RULES, VICE PRINCIPAL GRODD. WHAT RULE ARE YOU TALKING--
SORRY, SIR. I WILL ENSURE THESE NEW STUDENTS ARE NOT TARDY AGAIN.
YOU BETTER, BUMBLEBEE! IT IS YOUR DUTY AS AMBASSADOR TO NEW STUDENTS!

DETERMINE
TO DOMINATE
HURRY!
LIGHTEN UP, DOUBLE B.
YEAH, WHAT'S THE RUSH?
AND WHY DID VICE PRINCIPAL GRODD CALL YOU THE AMBASSADOR TO NEW STUDENTS?
YOU WERE THE AMBASSADOR *LAST* SEMESTER. I'M THE AMBASSADOR *NOW--*
YOU? GET REAL.
INFRARED. I CAN SCAN FOR HALL MONITORS.

CLASS!?! BUT I THOUGHT WE GOT OUT OF FOURTH PERIOD 'CUZ OF THE FIELD--
THIS HALL'S CLEAR. YOU SHOULD BE ABLE TO GET TO CLASS.
QUIET! YOU DON'T WANT PRINCIPAL SAVAGE CATCHING YOU.
I'M SORRY, BUT DID YOU SAY "*PRINCIPAL SAVAGE*"?
JOIN!
SAVAGE ARMY

CHAPTER THREE
SAVAGE HIGH

AVAGE ARMY
VANDAL SAVAGE? C'MON, HARLEY, YOU COULDN'T THINK OF A BETTER FAKE NAME FOR YOUR PRANK THAN THAT?
OF COURSE I COULD'VE!
BUT THIS ISN'T *MY* PRANK. IT'S BUMBLEBEE'S!
GOOD PRANK.
HARDY-HAR, DOUBLE B.
WAY TO MAKE US THINK THIS IS *"SAVAGE HIGH."*
UM, IT *IS* SAVAGE HIGH. WHO ARE YOU GUYS ANYWAY?

FOR THE LOVE OF ARMPIT FARTS! YA REALLY DON'T KNOW ANY OF US?
SHE KIND OF LOOKS LIKE A GIRL NAMED POWER GIRL, WHO GOES TO SCHOOL HERE.
THE GREEN TEAM SEEMS MORE LIKE THE GOTHAM CITY PREP TYPE.
WAIT. AREN'T YOU THE GIRL WHO GOT EXPELLED LAST SEMESTER FOR PUTTING KABOOM CANDY IN PRINCIPAL SAVAGE'S COFFEE?
TO DOMINATE
HA! NOT ME, BUT SOUNDS LIKE A GIRLIE AFTER MY OWN HEART!

I'VE DEFINITELY NEVER SEEN YOU BEFORE. WOULD'VE REMEMBERED THE TIARA.
BUMBLEBEE, IT'S ME, WONDER WOMAN. WE'RE BEST FRIENDS.
BEST FRIENDS?
BUT I DON'T HAVE ANY FRIENDS HERE.
THAT SETTLES IT! WE HAVE TO FIND MISS BELLE AND FIX THIS FUTURE!

WOOP!
WOOP!
HUH?
YEESH! THE CLASS BELL HERE SURE IS ANNOYIN'!
TO DOMINA
ANTI-SAVAGE INSURGENT IDENTIFIED ON SCHOOL GROUNDS. STUDENTS TO BATTLE STATIONS!
YOU GUYS HAVE TO GET OUT OF HERE!
TO DOMINAT
ANTI-SAVAGE INSURGENT? THAT MUST BE MISS BELLE!
I'LL GET YOU TO SAFETY.
BUT WE CAN'T LEAVE MISS BELLE BEHIND!

STOMP! STOMP! STOMP!

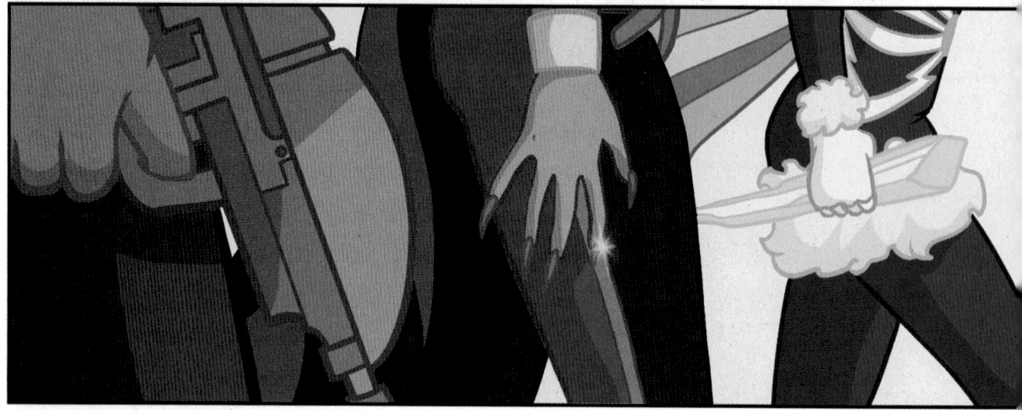

BUMBLEBEE! WHY AREN'T YOU GOING TO YOUR BATTLE STATION?
ON MY WAY, STAR SAPPHIRE!
BUT PRINCIPAL SAVAGE INSTRUCTED ME TO HANG HIS LATEST PROPAGANDA, I MEAN, **POSTER** FIRST.
PRINCIPAL SAVAGE INSTRUCTED? ALL RIGHT. AS YOU WERE.

HEY NOW, DOLLS! WHAT'S THE BIG IDEA?
THE BIG IDEA IS THAT YOU ORCHESTRATED A COUP AGAINST PRINCIPAL SAVAGE TWO MONTHS AGO!
YEAH, AND YOU JUST WALTZ IN HERE LIKE NOTHING HAPPENED.
GUESS THAT WAS REAL SILLY OF ME.
PRINCIPAL SAVAGE WILL BE WAITING FOR YOU IN INSURGENT DETENTION.
NO.
I HAVE TO HELP--
GO AFTER HER NOW, AND WE'LL *ALL* END UP IN DETENTION.
IF YOU WANT TO GET BACK TO YOUR RIGHT TIME--WHICH SOUNDS LIKE A GOOD TIME TO ME--WE HAVE TO *STRATEGIZE.*
YOU'RE RIGHT, BUMBLEBEE. AS USUAL.

I'VE NEVER BEEN IN HERE BEFORE.
IN OUR TIME, WE USE IT FOR DETECTIVE CLUB MEETINGS.
HOW TO FIX TIM
DETECTIVE CLUB? SOUNDS AWESOME! PRINCIPAL SAVAGE STRONGLY DISCOURAGES ANY INVESTIGATIVE WORK.
HOW TO FIX TIME BRAINSTORM
ALL RIGHT, WHO HAS AN IDEA?
ME ME ME!
BEAST BOY?
FIRST, WE NEED SIX DOZEN EXTRA CHEESY PIZZAS.
OH! IF WE'RE ORDERING PIZZA, CAN I GET GARLIC KNOTS?
NO PIZZA!
JUST THE GARLIC KNOTS THEN?
TO FIX TIME, WE NEED LIBERTY BELLE AND THE TIME MACHINE. HERE'S THE PLAN--
BRAINSTORM
"--HARLEY AND I WILL RECOVER THE TIME MACHINE."

"BUMBLEBEE, YOU LEAD WONDER WOMAN, SUPERGIRL, BEAST BOY, KATANA, AND IVY TO INSURGENT DETENTION AND RELEASE MISS BELLE."
STUDENT I.D. RECOGNIZED.
CLEARANCE AUTHORIZED.
INSURGENT DETENTION
UGH! I ALMOST PASSED THE LEVEL!
CHEETAH, WE'RE NOT SUPPOSED TO BE PLAYING GAMES WHILE ON DUTY.
SHUT IT, MAMMOTH!
HUH?
SHNK!
TRESPASSERS!

GET THEM!
YOU COULD USE A NAIL TRIM!
HISSSSS!
FORECAST IS LOOKING ICY!
INSURGENT DETENTION
I PREFER THE HEAT!
MAMMOTH, MEET *MY* MAMMOTH!
I ALWAYS WANTED TO STING THE BEE!
AAAGH!
BUT UNLIKE THE BEE, I CAN STING AGAIN AND AGAIN--

ZINK!
OW!
NO ONE HAS EVER HELPED ME BEFORE.
YOU BETTER START GETTING USED TO IT.
I THINK WE CAN GET IN OVER HERE!
CEASE OR THE TRAITOR KNOWN AS LIBERTY BELLE WILL BE IMMEDIATELY BOOM-TUBED TO THE PHANTOM ZONE!

WELCOME TO DETENTION.
GULP!
YOU INFILTRATORS MUST BE IN LEAGUE WITH *THE TWO.*
NO IDEA WHAT YOU'RE TALKING ABOUT, BUT THE *FOUR* OF US DEMAND TO BE RELEASED.

ZAAAP!
UNH!
ALL YOUR STRENGTH AND POWERS ARE USELESS IN THIS ROOM.
SCARY DUDE'S RIGHT. I CAN'T EVEN GO CHIMP!
WHERE ARE THE TWO?!
WE DON'T KNOW WHAT YOU'RE TALKING ABOUT.
IF YOU WON'T TALK TO ME ABOUT THE TWO, YOU WILL TALK TO MY FINEST INTERROGATOR. THE DEMON ETRIGAN.
CRICK CRACK!
PROFESSOR ETRIGAN?
BUT YOU DON'T DO THAT DEMON STUFF ANYMORE. YOU'RE A GOOD GUY!
HOW CAN YOUR WILD TALE OF REFORMATION BE TRUE, WHEN FOR CENTURIES IT'S BEEN VANDAL'S BIDDING I DO?
DID HE SAY "CENTURIES"?

AW, IT LOOKS LIKE WE HAVE A LEAK IN THE CHRONOLO-GEL TUBE. NO WAY THIS TIME MACHINE IS GOING ANYWHERE IN THIS SHAPE.
CAN YA FIX IT?
OF COURSE I CAN! JUST NEED THE RIGHT TOOLS.
HARLEY, WHAT'S THE STATUS INSIDE THE SHOP CLASS?
NOT LOOKING GOOD. DOC MAGNUS IS IN THERE. AND IT GETS WORSE--

HE'S MADE SOME UNFORTUNATE FACIAL HAIR DECISIONS.
WE'LL NEED TO CREATE A DISTRACTION TO GET HIM OUTTA THERE.
THIS TIMELINE'S HARLEY GAVE ME A REAL POPPIN' IDEA!
MECHANICS, ROBOTICS, AND AUTOMOTIVE WORKSHOP
KABOOM CANDY
FIRE IN THE HOLE!

KA-BOOOM!
WHAT THE NUTS AND BOLTS WAS THAT?!
VROOOOM
ALL DOORS LOCKED. NO ADMITTANCE ALLOWED.
WE HAVE A FEW MINUTES BEFORE DOC MAGNUS WILL BE ABLE TO OVERRIDE THAT.
WELL THEN, BATS, WE BETTER GET CRACKIN'!
I'LL GET CRACKING AND YOU KEEP A LOOKOUT.
YOU GOT IT.

ALL ACCESS POINTS TO THE DETENTION HALL HAVE BEEN CLOSED.
THEN WE'LL MAKE AN ACCESS POINT!
I HAVE MY LASSO OF TRUTH AND MY BULLETPROOF BRACELETS. ARE YOU CHARGED UP AND READY TO GO?
CHARGED, YES.
BUT I'M NOT READY. I'VE NEVER DONE ANYTHING LIKE THIS BEFORE. I DON'T KNOW IF I CAN.
I KNOW YOU CAN. THE BUMBLEBEE I KNOW HAS DONE IT BEFORE.

YOU'RE CAPABLE OF AMAZING THINGS. I'VE SEEN YOU STAND UP AGAINST GIGANTA, SOLOMON GRUNDY AND CROC!
NO WAY! I TOOK DOWN CROC?
HE WAS TRYING TO STEAL A TUNA SANDWICH FROM THE CAPES & COWLS CAFÉ AND YOU STOPPED HIM BEFORE HE EVEN KNEW WHAT HIT HIM!
THAT GREATNESS HAS ALWAYS BEEN INSIDE OF YOU. YOU JUST HAVE TO BELIEVE IN YOUR SUPER SELF.
BELIEVE IN MY SUPER SELF.
THEY CUT OFF ALL REGULAR ACCESS, BUT THEY DIDN'T COUNT ON A BEE-SIZED HERO.

THAT SHOULD DO IT.
HMMM. SOMETHING'S STILL OFF.
TAP! TAP!
I NEED MISS BELLE. SHE'S THE ONLY ONE WHO KNOWS HOW TO WORK THIS THING.

HOW'S IT LOOKIN' IN THERE?
NOT GREAT.
DIDN'T I ASK YOU TO KEEP A LOOKOUT?
YA SURE DID! AND WE BETTER LOOK OUT 'CUZ DOC MAGNUS IS HEADED OUR WAY.
HEY! WHO ARE YOU KIDS AND WHAT ARE YOU DOING IN MY CLASSROOM?!
SHAKE A LEG! *TIME* IS OF THE ESSENCE!

NO! IT'S ***NOT READY!***
OH MY COGS! WHAT A FASCINATING PIECE OF MACHINERY!
WHERE ***ARE*** WE?
OOPSIE-POOPSIES!
SCHOOL BUS
PLUNK!

CHAPTER FOUR
HARLEY & BATGIRL'S
EXCELLENT ADVENTURE

I WAS JUST TRYIN' TO GET AWAY FROM THAT MADCAP MAGNUS.
HARLEY, DID YOU SEND US TO THE FUTURE?
AND NOW THAT WE'RE SAFE, LET'S GET BACK INSIDE AND PUT THIS ***DISTURBINGLY DESERTED*** FUTURE IN THE REAR VIEW!
UH-OH. NOT SO DESERTED!
TROMP! TROMP! TROMP!

HALT!
THIS DISTRICT BELONGS TO THE ATOMIC KNIGHTS!
LEAVE US ALONE!
DON'TCHA WORRY, BATS!
THIS IS NOTHING HARLEY QUINN'S WINNIN' PERSONALITY CAN'T TAKE CARE OF!
GREETINGS, YA BIG OL' ATOMIC KNIGHTS! WE COME IN--

SOON...
WE FOUND THESE GIRLS IN THE UNAUTHORIZED ZONE.
I HAVE A HANDCUFF-LOCK PICKER IN MY UTILITY BELT.
JUST DON'T TIP THEM OFF UNTIL WE'RE READY TO FIGHT OUR WAY OUT.
THEY DON'T HAVE HOLO-PERMITS OR I.D. CHIPS.
CLICK!
WE MUST ASSUME THE TRESPASSERS ARE SPIES FOR VANDAL SAVAGE!
WE'RE NOT NO STINKIN' SPIES! VANDAL SAVAGE IS THE FELLA WE'RE TRYING TO STOP!
SHE ESCAPED THE HANDCUFFS?!

DOGS, GET THEM!
BARK!
BARK!
BARK!
GOOD DOGGIE!
WOW.
I GOTS A GIFT WITH THE POOCHES. UM...AND HYENAS!
OUR DOGS ARE FINE JUDGES OF CHARACTER, GARDNER.
YOU'RE RIGHT, MARENE. THE GIRLS' STORY MUST BE TRUE.
HOW DID YOU GET TO THE UNAUTHORIZED ZONE?
TIME TRAVEL GOOF.
WHAT YEAR IS IT, ANYWAY?
CLICK!
THE YEAR? 2150.
THAT CAN'T BE RIGHT! WE MET VANDAL SAVAGE BACK IN 2016.
BY 2150, HE SHOULD'VE KICKED THE BUCKET!

YOU REALLY DON'T KNOW? YOU'VE NEVER SEEN THE HOLO-STORY?
SEEN IT? I DON'T EVEN KNOW WHAT IT IS!
FOR YEARS, THIS STORY PLAYED ON EVERY HOLO-VISION THROUGHOUT THE GALAXY.
THE GRAND STORY OF
VANDAL SAVAGE
VANDAL SAVAGE WAS THE GREATEST CAVEMAN WHO EVER LIVED!
OVER FIFTY THOUSAND YEARS AGO,THE BRIGHT AND CUNNING VANDAL SAVAGE SAW A METEORITE FALL FROM THE SKY.

BEING BRAVER AND BOLDER THAN OTHER CAVEMEN, VANDAL SAVAGE TRACKED THE METEORITE.
THE INSURGENTS CLAIM THAT IT WAS THE METEORITE'S RADIATION THAT GAVE VANDAL SAVAGE HIS SUPERHUMAN POWERS AND MADE HIM IMMORTAL.
BUT WE KNOW THE HEAVENS BESTOWED THESE POWERS ON VANDAL SAVAGE BECAUSE HE WAS THE ONLY HUMAN WORTHY OF RULING THE GALAXY.
SAVAGE HIGH
IT TOOK VANDAL SAVAGE MANY MILLENNIA TO REALIZE HIS CALLING AND GATHER HIS SUPREME ARMY AT SAVAGE HIGH SCHOOL.

THE WEAK INSURGENTS FOOLISHLY FOUGHT, BUT THEY WERE CRUSHED BY THE STRENGTH AND POWER OF THE SAVAGE ARMY.
ATTACK! USE ALL YOUR SUPER-POWERS!
VANDAL SAVAGE, THE GALAXY'S GREATEST EMPEROR!
ALL HAIL EMPEROR VANDAL SAVAGE!

HERE AT OUR METROPOLIS BASE, THE ATOMIC KNIGHTS STILL STAND AGAINST SAVAGE. BUT WE ARE DWINDLING.
-GASP!- THIS IS OUR FAULT. WE MESSED WITH TIME.
BUT THIS DOESN'T MAKE A LICK OF SENSE!
THAT SAID THIS SAVAGE FELLA GOT HIS POWERS FROM A METEORITE FIFTY THOUSAND YEARS AGO.
BUT ONE MISSIN' DINO EGG FROM THE JURASSIC ERA COULDN'T'VE CAUSED A METEORITE!

YOU TOOK A DINO EGG? THIS IS ALL YOUR FAULT!
MAYBE I DID TAKE A MEASLY LITTLE EGG, BUT **NO WAY** THIS WHOLE RIGMAROLE'S MY FAULT!
REMOVING SOMETHING SMALL FROM THE PAST CAN CHANGE THE FUTURE IN BIG WAYS--WHICH YOU WOULD HAVE KNOWN IF YOU WERE LISTENING TO MISS BELLE!
WELL, IF YOU'RE SO GREAT AT FIXING EVERYTHING, THEN WHY DON'T YOU FIX THIS?
I WOULDN'T HAVE TO FIX EVERYTHING IF YOU DIDN'T RUIN EVERYTHING!
RUIN EVERYTHING?
C'MON. LET'S GET BACK TO THE TIME MACHINE AND GET THAT EGG WHERE IT BELONGS.
UM, GOOD LUCK!

WHERE'S THE EGG?
ER, IN MY BACKPACK.
WHICH IS?
BACK AT SAVAGE HIGH.
UGH!

WE'LL GO BACK TO SAVAGE HIGH, GET THAT EGG, AND FIX THE PAST, ONCE AND FOR ALL.
SCHOOL BUS
1950 A.D.
1940 A.D.
1914.
HERO HIGH
THIS DOESN'T LOOK RIGHT.
NO SAVAGE HIGH HERE.
HEY! YOUR JALOPY CUT DOWN MY KITE!
WAIT A TICK--AREN'T YOU AMELIA EARHART?
HOW'D YA KNOW MY NAME?
YOU'RE THE FIRST FEMALE AVIATOR TO FLY SOLO ACROSS THE ATLANTIC!
FLYIN' PLANES? HA! EVERYBODY KNOWS THAT GIRLS CAN'T FLY PLANES.

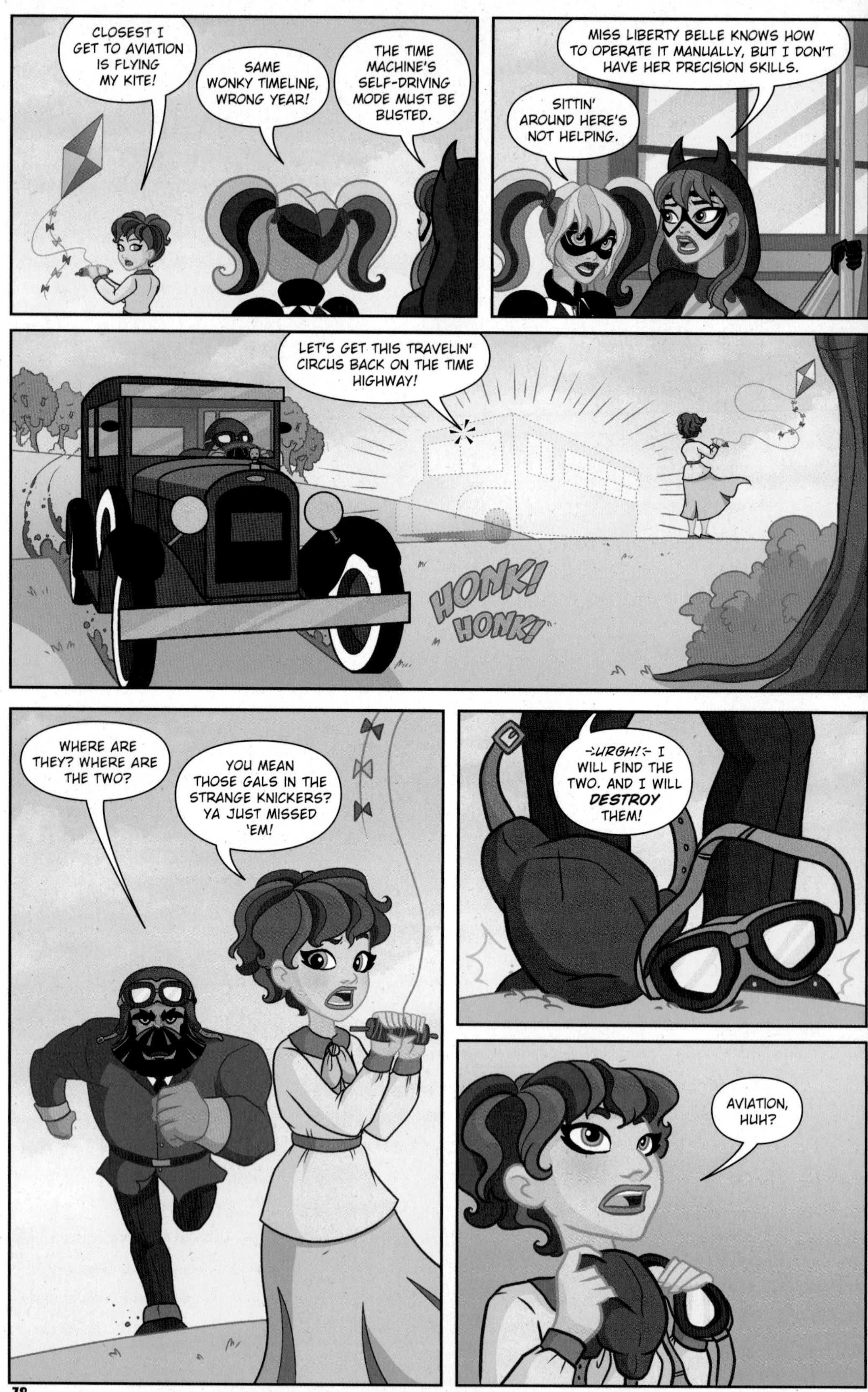
CLOSEST I GET TO AVIATION IS FLYING MY KITE!
SAME WONKY TIMELINE, WRONG YEAR!
THE TIME MACHINE'S SELF-DRIVING MODE MUST BE BUSTED.
MISS LIBERTY BELLE KNOWS HOW TO OPERATE IT MANUALLY, BUT I DON'T HAVE HER PRECISION SKILLS.
SITTIN' AROUND HERE'S NOT HELPING.
LET'S GET THIS TRAVELIN' CIRCUS BACK ON THE TIME HIGHWAY!
HONK! HONK!
WHERE ARE THEY? WHERE ARE THE TWO?
YOU MEAN THOSE GALS IN THE STRANGE KNICKERS? YA JUST MISSED 'EM!
-URGH!- I WILL FIND THE TWO. AND I WILL DESTROY THEM!
AVIATION, HUH?

HI! COULD YOU TELL US WHAT YEAR IT IS?
OH, I'M NOT SUPPOSED TO TALK TO STRANGERS.
HARLEY QUINN, AT YOUR SERVICE.
I'M EMILY DICKINSON. AND NOW THAT WE'RE DULY MET, THE YEAR IS 1847.
EMILY DICKINSON! WELL, "I'M NOBODY! WHO ARE YOU?"
I JUST TOLD YOU, MISS NOBODY. AND IF YOU DON'T MIND, YOU INTERRUPTED ME.
LET ME GUESS--YOU WERE IN THE MIDDLE OF WRITIN' POEMS?
WRITING? GOODNESS NO! A PROPER LADY DOES NOT WHILE AWAY HER DAYS WITH FRIVOLOUS POETRY!
THEY'VE BEEN HERE! I KNOW IT!
SORRY, I'M NOT SUPPOSED TO TALK TO STRANGERS.

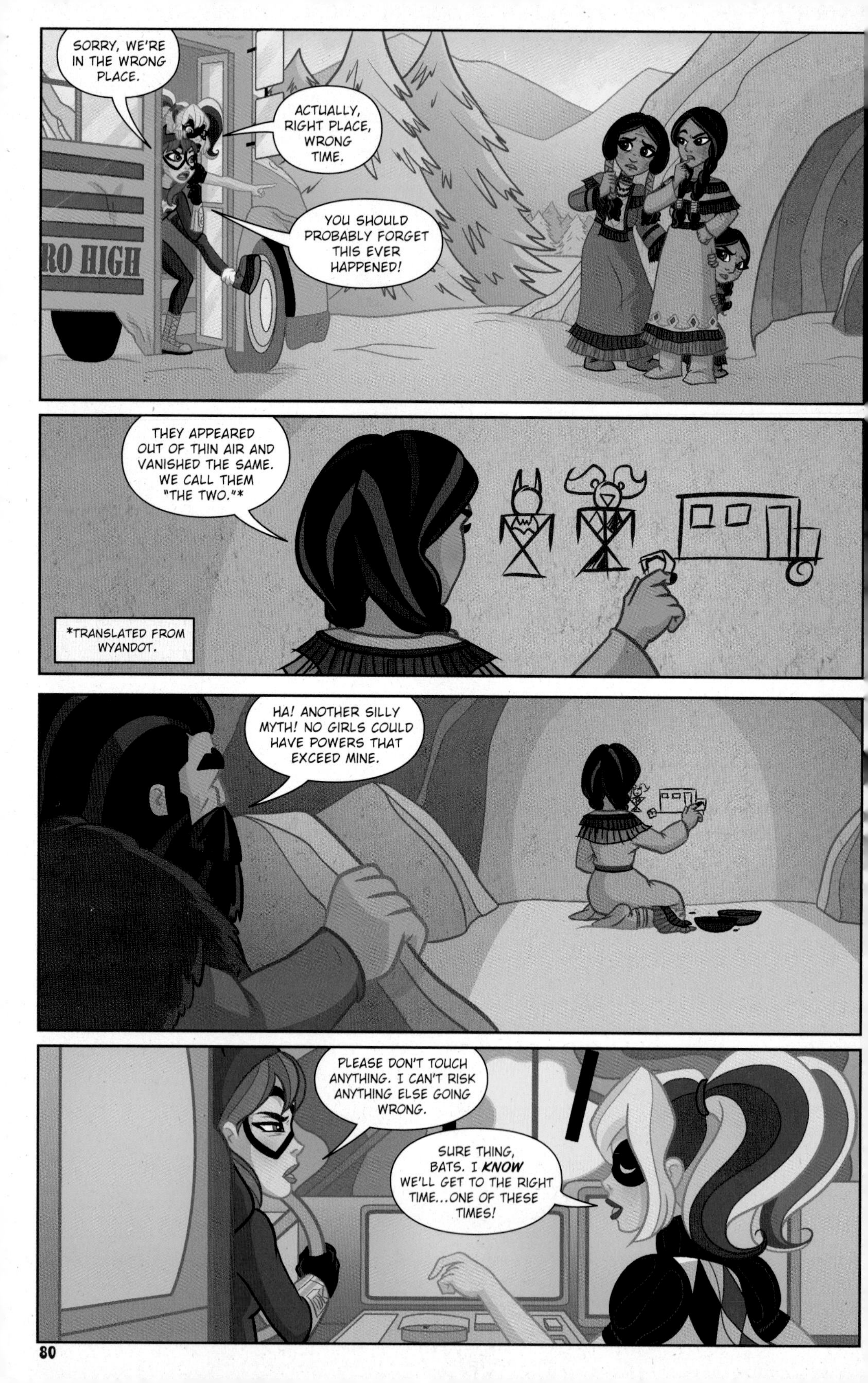
SORRY, WE'RE IN THE WRONG PLACE.
ACTUALLY, RIGHT PLACE, WRONG TIME.
YOU SHOULD PROBABLY FORGET THIS EVER HAPPENED!
RO HIGH
THEY APPEARED OUT OF THIN AIR AND VANISHED THE SAME. WE CALL THEM "THE TWO."*
*TRANSLATED FROM WYANDOT.
HA! ANOTHER SILLY MYTH! NO GIRLS COULD HAVE POWERS THAT EXCEED MINE.
PLEASE DON'T TOUCH ANYTHING. I CAN'T RISK ANYTHING ELSE GOING WRONG.
SURE THING, BATS. I ***KNOW*** WE'LL GET TO THE RIGHT TIME...ONE OF THESE TIMES!

WHEN DO YOU THINK WE ARE?
WITCHES! BURN THEM!
WHENEVER IT IS, IT'S TIME TO GET OUT OF HERE!
SCHOOL BUS
HIGH
THE TWO? THE OLD LEGEND IS TRUE!
GET THE WITCHES!
THEY DISAPPEARED!
ALL YE STAY BACK, LEST YE TOUCH THEIR WITCHY RESIDUE!
THE TWO MUST BE IMMORTAL LIKE ME. I WILL FIND THE SOURCE OF THEIR POWERS AND TAKE IT FOR MYSELF!

SAVAGE HIGH SCHOOL, 2017.
WHEN WE GET OUTTA HERE, I'M NEVER TAKING BURRITOS FOR GRANTED AGAIN!
I WISH BATGIRL WERE HERE.
I MEAN, I DON'T WISH SHE WERE STUCK WITH US, BUT I MISS HER.
I MISS THE SMELL OF ROSES, AND GRASS, AND PINECONES!
MY KNUCKLES MISS THE SENSATION OF PUNCHING A BAD GUY.
BUMBLEBEE STING!
ZZAP!
KABLAM!
AND THERE ARE A WHOLE LOT OF BAD GUYS I WANT TO PUNCH--
SOMEONE DESTROYED THE POWER DRAINERS!
KABLAM!
KABLAM!
KABLAM!
SUPER STRENGTH AT FULL FORCE!
LET'S GET OUT OF HERE!

GROAN!
WONDER WOMAN, YOU SAVED US!
NOT ME-- IT WAS BUMBLEBEE WHO DID THE HARD PART.
HEY!
AW, IT WAS JUST A LITTLE GETTING LITTLE AND A FEW ELECTRIC STINGS!
WAY TO GO, DOUBLE B!
YOU'RE BETTER THAN BEGONIAS!
ÜBERFLY MOVES, GIRL!
C'MON! YOUR TEACHER WILL BE THIS WAY.
WE'RE COMING, MISS BELLE!

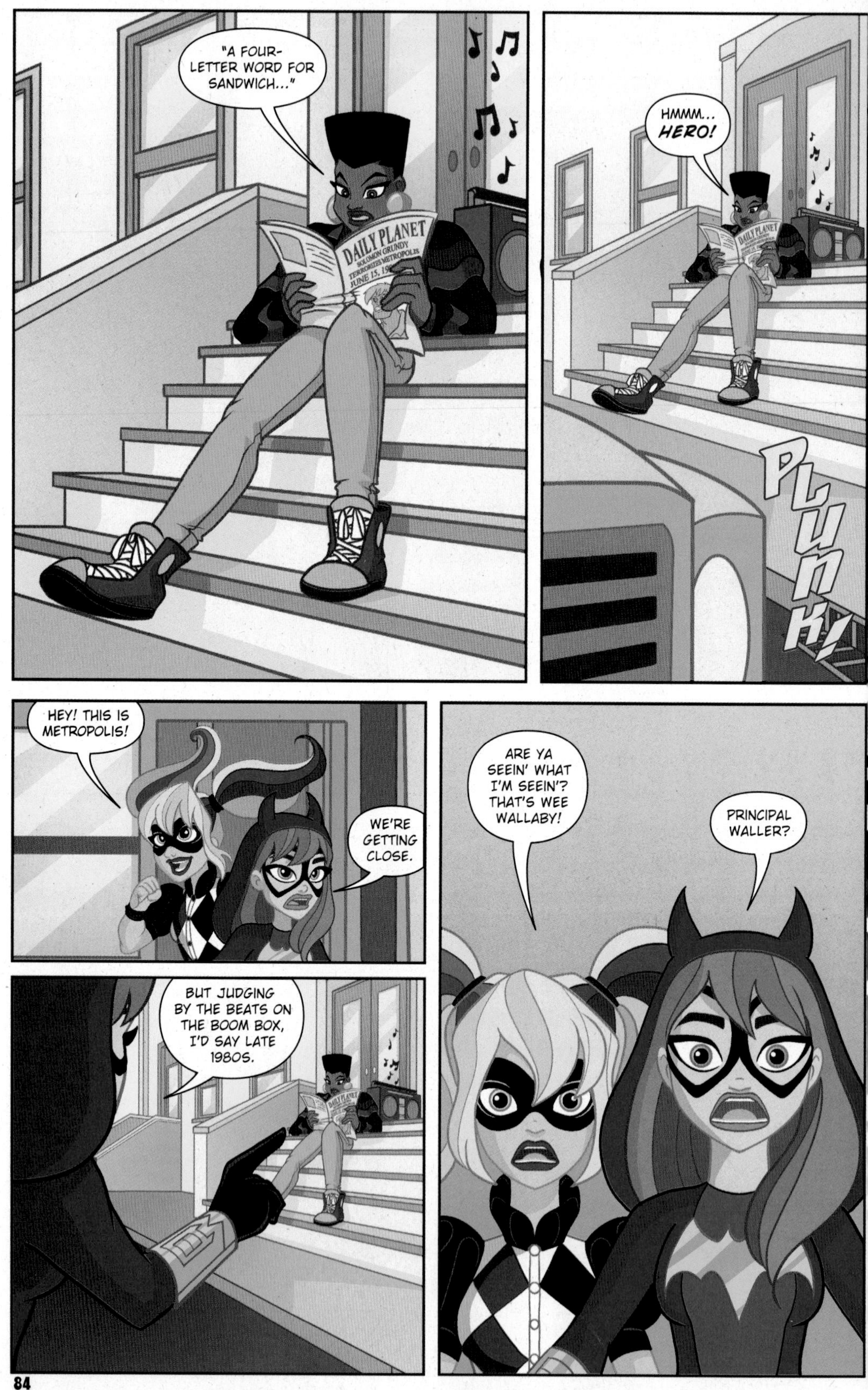
"A FOUR-LETTER WORD FOR SANDWICH..."
DAILY PLANET
SOLOMON GRUNDY TERRORIZES METROPOLIS
HMMM... *HERO!*
PLUNK!
HEY! THIS IS METROPOLIS!
WE'RE GETTING CLOSE.
BUT JUDGING BY THE BEATS ON THE BOOM BOX, I'D SAY LATE 1980S.
ARE YA SEEIN' WHAT I'M SEEIN'? THAT'S WEE WALLABY!
PRINCIPAL WALLER?

SOLOMON GRUNDY, BORN ON A MONDAY--
-AAGH!- MONSTER!
NO, HARLEY! WE CAN'T INTERFERE!
WE GOTTA HELP HER! THAT'S WHAT SHE TAUGHT US TO DO!
BUT SHE HASN'T TAUGHT US THAT IN THE 1980S.
WE KNOW WALLER GOT THROUGH THIS BEFORE WITHOUT US. IF WE INTERFERE, WE MIGHT MESS UP HER FUTURE!
RIGHT. WALLY'S GOT THIS. I WON'T RUIN IT.
HERO HIGH
HELP! SOMEONE, HELP!
GRUNDY GET GIRL!

WE MADE IT TO SAVAGE HIGH!
HIGH
PLUNK!
WE'LL HAVE THIS TIME TROUBLE FIXED IN A FLASH!
THE TWO! I'VE BEEN TRACKING YOU FOR CENTURIES, BUT NOW YOUR TIME IS UP!

CHAPTER FIVE
EGGING ON

GET THEM!
WHAT'S THE PLAN, BATS?
WE, UM...
FIGHT!
NO THROWING WEAPONS AT YOUR SUPERIORS!
MEET MY GOO GRENADE!
BOOM!
THAT WAS UNCHARACTERISTICALLY UNFASHIONABLE OF YA, MR. CRAZY QUILT!

BOOM! BOOM!
WHAT WAS THAT?
JUMPING JUNIPERS!
JOIN!
ARMY
DETERMINE
TO DOMINATE
DETERMINE
TO DOMINATE
I'VE GOT A FEELING PRINCIPAL SAVAGE FOUND YOUR FRIENDS.
AY-YI-YI-YI-YIIIIII!
UH-OH.
IT'S SEVEN TEACHERS VERSUS THE TWO OF THEM.
TIME TO EVEN THE ODDS.

TIME TO TEACH THESE, UM, TEACHERS A LESSON!
THANKS A BAJILLION, WONDY!
HEY, RED TORNADO, GUESS WHO ACED HER FLYING TEST?
YOUR QUERY DOES NOT COMPUTE.
THIS IS FOR ALL THOSE TIMES YOU PUT ME IN DETENTION!
GRRRR!
I DARE YOU TO COME NEAR. YOUR SCREAMS I LONG TO HEAR.
WHOA! WATCH THE NAILS, PROFESSOR!
SLASH!
HURRY! GO GET THAT DINO EGG!
ON IT LIKE A SONNET!

ALL RIGHT, OLD-TIMER, LET'S GET YOU FIXED UP!
HEY, WATCH THE PAINT!
SCHOOL BUS
C'MON, SWEETHEART, YOU CAN'T BEAT ME. I'M A MASTER OF BOXING, MUAY THAI, CAPOEIRA, KRAV--
OOPS, I GOT BORED WITH YOU LISTING ALL THE MARTIAL ARTS I'VE MASTERED.
NGH!
AND THE NAME'S KATANA, NOT "SWEETHEART."
UH-UH-UH...
KACHUNK! KACHUNK!
NOW THIS REALLY GRINDS MY GEARS.

FINALLY A CHANCE TO TRY OUT MY NEW METAL MEN!
ATTACK!
KACHUNK! KACHUNK! KACHUNK!
TAKE THIS, YOU HUNK OF JUNK!
BAM!
RELEASE ME!
SORRY, ROBO-MAN, BUT MY MAMA TOLD ME NOT TO LISTEN TO HEAVY METAL!
KRANG!

ELECTRIC BEE STING DODGE SUCCESSFUL.
DODGE THIS!
HUH?
LASSO DODGE SUCCESSFUL.
WELL DONE, PLATINUM! I CAN'T WAIT TO SEE WHAT YOU CAN DO WHEN THE RESPONSOMETERS ARE COMPLETE!
WHAT SHOULD WE DO, BATGIRL?
THE DOC MAGNUS I KNOW TAUGHT US THAT ROBOTS CAN BE DEFEATED WITH AN ELECTROMAGNETIC PULSE ATTACK.

BOMBS AWAY!
LET'S SCRAMBLE SOME ROBOT BRAIN!
WHAT IS--
ZZZZZZZRRRR...
BOOM!

ESE TEACHERS
GHT US HOW TO
IGHT, RIGHT?
YEAH! I GET WHERE YOU'RE GOING!
AND THAT IS?
LET'S HIT 'EM WITH THEIR BEST ADVICE!
PROFESSOR ETRIGAN TAUGHT ME THE IMPORTANCE OF A DRAMATIC ENTRANCE!
OOF!
MR. CRAZY QUILT IS ALL ABOUT HAVING AN
BER-AWESOME SUPER-SUIT--
AND EXPLOITING THE FLAWS OF YOUR ENEMY'S LACKLUSTER STYLE!
OOOOO! WEDGIE!
I LEARNED FROM RED TORNADO HOW TO FIGHT WHILE FLYING!
THIS IS WITHOUT PRECEDENT!
MY MAIN MAN, COACH WILDCAT, SHOWED ME HOW TO UNLEASH MY INNER BEAST!

-NGH!-
BECAUSE I WON'T LET THE FUTURE BE LIKE THAT!
WHY HAVE YOU BEEN FOLLOWING ME?
OOF!
YOU'VE SEEN THE FUTURE.
UM, I MEANT TO SAY--
YOU KNOW I WIN!
IT'S OVER, LITTLE GIRL. YOU CAN'T CHANGE THE PAST, AND I WON'T GIVE YOU THE CHANCE TO CHANGE THE FUTURE.

-PHEW!-
MY BACKPACK'S
STILL INTACT!
BUT...
...MY DINO
EGG ISN'T.
-ULP!-

BABY DINO? WHERE YA AT?!
DINO?!
DON'T YOU JUST LOVE PRINCIPAL SAVAGE'S PLAN TO TAKE OVER THE WORLD?
IT'S PURR-FECT!
SO COOL!
NOT HERE.
GIVE UP? THE DOCTOR IS HIS MOTHER!
OOOOH. GOOD RIDDLE, RIDDLER.
WHERE ARE YA, ITTY-BITTY BEASTY?

AWRIGHT, HARLS. YOU GOTTA PUT YOUR BRAIN BUCKET INTO OVERDRIVE, CHANNEL YOUR INNER MARY ANNING, SÉANCE WITH YOUR SUBCONSCIOUS SCIENTIST!
IF I WERE A FRESHLY HATCHED PTERODACTYL, WHERE WOULD I GO?
SKREE!
Cafeteria
SKREE!
I'M COMING FOR YA, BABE!
SKREE?

AW, LI'L PUDDIN'! I CAN'T LET YA TIME TRAVEL ON AN EMPTY STOMACH!
ZZZZZOOM! CAPTAIN SLOPPY JOE REQUESTIN' CLEARANCE TO LAND!
CHOMP!
YOWZA! CAPTAIN SLOPPY JOE, WE HARDLY KNEW YA!
BURPP!
WOOF! LET'S GET YOU BACK HOME BEFORE I GOTTA CHANGE ANY DIAPERS.

SKREE?
I WAS JUST TEASIN'. I'D CHANGE ALL THE DINO DIAPERS IN THE WORLD IF I COULD KEEP YA--BUT, OL' SMARTY-BATS IS RIGHT.
YOU BELONG IN THE PAST AND I'M GOING TO MAKE SURE YOU GET THERE.
NO MATTER WHAT, I'M NOT GONNA RUIN THINGS THIS TIME.

YEAH, I'VE SEEN THE FUTURE AND THE REBELS ARE GOING TO TAKE YOU--
HUH?
SK
SKREE!
GET HIM, BITEY MCPUDDIN'-FACE!
GET OFF ME, YOU SLIMY REPTILE!
SKREE! SKREE!
AAAAAGH!

SKREE!
BATS! GRAB ON!
I GOT YA, GIRLIE!
TELESCOPING MALLET HANDLE? NICE!
YIIIIIII!
IS THAT THE PTERODACTYL FROM THE EGG?
SURE IS.
WOW, YOU ARE REALLY GOOD WITH DINOS.
WHAT CAN I SAY? BITEY AND I HIT IT OFF!
WE BETTER GET OUT BEFORE SAVAGE GETS UP.
GROAN!

SHAKE A LEG, KIDS!
ERO HIGH
SCHOOL BUS
BUMBLEBEE, C'MON!
I CAN'T. YOUR TIME ISN'T MY TIME.
BUT, MISS BELLE, BUMBLEBEE HAS TO COME WITH US! WE CAN'T LEAVE HER HERE!
THAT'S THE RULES OF TIME TRAVEL.
BUT ONCE THE RIFT IN TIME IS HEALED, AND THIS TIMELINE CEASES TO EXIST, THIS BUMBLEBEE WILL MERGE WITH OUR OWN BUMBLEBEE.
I'M SORRY.
IT'S ALL RIGHT. TWO BUMBLEBEES IN ONE TIMELINE WOULD BE WAY TOO MUCH SWEETNESS FOR THE WORLD TO HANDLE.

THANKS FOR BEING MY FRIEND. I ALWAYS WANTED A FRIEND LIKE YOU.
LIKE ME? I LEARNED HOW TO BE A FRIEND FROM YOU.
BEST FRIENDS FOREVER. NO MATTER WHAT TIMELINE THAT "FOREVER" IS.
SEE YA SOON, BESTIE!

HURRY UP, WONDER WOMAN!
GET OUT OF HERE.
STOP THEM!
I'LL HOLD THEM OFF!
I WON'T LET YOU *HURT* MY FRIENDS!
ZAP!
ZAP!
ZAP!

AW, HE'S SO CUTE!
YEAH, NOT TO MENTION BRAVE, HEROIC, AND WITH A BITIN' SENSE OF HUMOR.
ZZZZZZ...
70,000 BC
HERE WE ARE! BACK TO THE JURASSIC ERA!
YES! WE MADE IT!
PLUNK!
SCHOOL BUS
NOT TO RAIN ON Y'ALL'S PARADE, BUT IS ANYONE ELSE CONCERNED ABOUT THE FACT THAT WE'RE ABOUT TO FALL OVER THE EDGE OF A CLIFF?

CHAPTER SIX
DÉJÀ VU

AAAAAGH!
SCHOOL BUS
I GOT YOU!
SCHOOL BUS
GOING UP!
SWEET SAVE, SUPERGIRL!

WELL, PUDDIN', IT'S TIME TO GET YA HOME.
I'M COMING WITH YOU!
OF COURSE YA ARE. GOTTA MAKE SURE I DON'T FUMBLE IT.
ALL RIGHT, HARLEY, THE DINO'S BACK IN PLACE SO THE TIMELINE SHOULD BE CORRECT. LET'S GET TO THE FUTURE.
YA WERE A GOOD EGG AND AN EVEN BETTER BABY.
SKREE!
BUT YA DON'T BELONG IN MY TIME. YA GOTTA BE BACK HERE TO STOP VANDAL SAVAGE.
HOW DO YOU THINK HE'LL DO THAT, ANYWAY?
WELL, I WAS THINKING...

"MAYBE ONE DAY, BITEY'LL MEET A LITTLE CRITTER...
"AND FOR ONE REASON OR ANOTHER, HE WON'T EAT THAT CRITTER...
"AND THAT CRITTER WILL HAVE BABIES AND THE BABIES WILL HAVE BABIES AND SO ON AND SO FORTH FOR MILLIONS OF YEARS!
"ALL THE WAY UNTIL WE GET TO OUR NEMESIS, VANDAL SAVAGE."

ME WANT BIG BEASTIE!
"AND SOMEHOW, THAT GREAT-TO-THE-HUNDREDTH-DEGREE-GRANDBABY CRITTER HAPPENS TO DISTRACT SAVAGE...
BAM!
"SO HE DOESN'T MAKE IT TO THE METEOR TO BREATHE ALL THOSE VAPORS THAT MAKE HIM IMMORTAL..."
GRRRRRR!
EEEEE! ME SORRY!
"...AND WE CAN ALL LIVE HAPPILY EVER AFTER!"

SOUNDS ABOUT RIGHT TO ME.
GUESS IT'S TIME TO SAY GOOD-BYE.
BYE, BATS. HAVE A NICE FUTURE.
HARLEY, WHAT ARE YOU TALKING ABOUT?
I WANT TO STAY HERE WITH THE DINOS, WHERE I CAN'T RUIN EVERYTHING.
I DIDN'T MEAN IT.
IT SURE FELT LIKE YOU DID.

I WAS JUST UPSET THAT YOU TOOK THE EGG.
WELL, I TOOK IT 'CUZ I WANTED TO BE THE BEST AT SOMETHIN'.
I KNOW I CAN'T OUT-FLY WONDY OR OUT-GROW IVY OR OUT-EYE-LASER SUPES.
BUT I THOUGHT I WAS PRETTY GOOD AT DINOS...UNTIL *YOU* CAME ALONG.
I KNOW YOU THINK IT'S SILLY, BUT I FIGURED IF I HAD MY OWN 'DACTYL, I COULD PROVE I WAS THE BEST AT DINOS.
I DON'T THINK IT'S SILLY. I GET IT--
HOW COULD YA? YOU'RE THE BEST AT VEHICLES, 'PUTERS, BUILDIN' BAT BUNKERS, AND SAVIN' THE DAY! AND I'M JUST FAIR-TO-MIDDLIN' HARLEY, ***RUINING EVERYTHING.***

I'M SORRY. REALLY SORRY. IF I COULD GO BACK IN TIME AND TAKE BACK SAYING THAT, I WOULD.
BUT WE ALL KNOW HOW TERRIBLE I AM AT TIME TRAVEL.
HA! I GUESS WE DID FIND ONE THING YOU WEREN'T GREAT AT.
I THINK YOU'RE GREAT AT LOTS OF THINGS, LIKE ACROBATICS AND MAKING PEOPLE LAUGH, AND STEALING DINO EGGS WITHOUT ME SUSPECTING--
YEAH, POINT HARLEY!
AND I THINK YOU ARE BETTER AT DINOS THAN ME.
AW, SHUCKS!
ZZZZZZZZ

GOOD WORK, HARLEY.
SKREE!
RIGHT BACK ATCHA, BATS.
DIDJA GALS GET IT BACK ALL PROPER?
SURE DID!
NOW EVERYTHING'S JUST HUNKY-DORY!

HOME SWEET HOME!
PLUNK!
AW, SUCCULENT SUPER HERO HIGH VEGETATION!
BACK ALREADY? I HAVEN'T EVEN STARTED MY FIELD TRIP MAKEUP REPORT YET!
IT'S YOU! IT'S REALLY YOU!
YEAH, IT'S ME. WHO ELSE WOULD IT BE?
DAD! DO YOU KNOW WHO VANDAL SAVAGE IS?
SCHOO
VANDAL SAVAGE? CAN'T SAY I'M FAMILIAR WITH THE NAME. IS HE IN ONE OF THOSE BOY BANDS?
THAT'S THE RIGHT ANSWER!
IF I KNEW NOT KNOWING THINGS GOT ME HUGS, I WOULD NOT KNOW MORE OFTEN! NOW I BETTER GO LET PRINCIPAL FOX KNOW YOU'VE SAFELY RETURNED.

PRINCIPAL FOX?!
NOT PRINCIPAL WALLER?! YOU'VE GOT TO BE KIDDING ME!
MAYBE IT'S NOT WHAT WE DID WRONG, BUT WHAT WE DIDN'T DO AT ALL.
WHAT DID WE DO WRONG THIS TIME?!
EXCUSE US, EVERYONE! HARLEY AND I HAVE ONE LAST THING TO TAKE CARE OF!
HOLY HYENAS! YOU REALLY WANT ME TO GO WITH YOU?
OF COURSE! NO ONE CAN DO THIS BETTER THAN YOU!

1914.
HEY, AMELIA!
HERO HIGH
STILL FLYIN' THAT KITE, HUH?
NOT JUST FLYING A KITE--I'M STUDYING THE AERONAUTICAL MOVEMENT OF THE KITE IN SPACE.
Y'SEE, THERE'S SOMETHING ABOUT FLYING THAT SPEAKS TO ME.
POW! AVIATION PIONEERING ON!
YEAH, BABY!

1847.
I SPY AN EMILY DICKINSON WRITIN'!
INDEED. A FRIEND GAVE ME THIS BOOK OF POEMS, AND I'VE BEEN QUITE INSPIRED!
POW! POETRY ON!
IF THE REST OF HISTORY'S RIGHT, THERE'S ONLY ONE PLACE THAT WALLY'S TIMELINE COULD'VE GONE TOPSY-TURVY.
JUNE 15, 1
IT'S TIME TO SAVE PRE-PRINCIPAL WALLER!

PLUNK!
"A FOUR-LETTER WORD FOR SANDWICH..."
DAILY PLANET
HMMM... HERO!
SOLOMON GRUNDY, BORN ON A MONDAY--
AAGH! MONSTER!
WE GOT A GRUMBLIN' GRUNDY THAT NEEDS TAKIN' DOWN A NOTCH!
POW! HERO ON!
REAL-LIFE SUPER HEROES? RAD!

AAAGH!
NO LITTLE GIRLS MESS WITH SOLOMON GRUNDY!
CRASH!
OOF!
HA! ONE PIN SHORT OF THE STRIKE!
NGH!
OOH, GRUNDY WITH THE SPARE!
CRASH!

LET GO OF ME, YOU SMELLY, OVERSIZE SWAMP MONSTER!
I'LL GET HIM--
HARLEY, WAIT!
BUT I THOUGHT YA TRUSTED ME NOW?
I DO. BUT I DON'T TRUST THE BANANA PEEL ON YOUR HEAD.

LET'S SAVE THIS DAY!
ZZSSH!
COME AT ME, SLOW-MO BRO!
GRUNDY, THIS PATH IS A DEAD END!
HEY, BATTER, BATTER, SWING!
TAKE THAT!

GROAN.
THANKS FOR SAVING ME!
GIRL, YA GOT MOVES!
YEAH, THAT WAS SOME BONA FIDE HERO WORK, UM, MISS WALLER!
MISS WALLER? YOU CAN CALL ME AMANDA.
HA HA HA HA HA!
SORRY, I JUST NEVER IMAGINED YA HAVING A FIRST NAME BEFORE!
AND THINK OF THE DETENTION WE'D GET IF WE ACTUALLY CALLED HER "AMANDA."
IT'D BE WORSE THAN THE TIME I GLITTER BOMBED THE FACULTY LOUNGE! GRODD'S STILL PICKIN' GLITTER OUT OF HIS FUR!

WAIT! WILL I EVER SEE YOU GUYS AGAIN?
YOU CAN COUNT ON IT!
JUST REMEMBER THREE LITTLE WORDS-- SUPER HERO HIGH!
HIG
HERE IT IS. THE MOMENT OF TRUTHINESS!
PLUNK!
THAT'S OUR PRINCIPAL!
YEAH, BABY!
PRINCIPAL WALLER

RRRRRRRINNNGGGG!
WAY TO GO, BRO!
AND THEN I BECAME KING OF THE DINOSAURS!
YOU EXPERIENCED MUCH AMAZINGNESS ON THE TRIP OF FIELDING.
I'M NEVER TIME TRAVELING AGAIN!
NEXT TIME STAY HERE WITH ME!
THAT'S SO COOL! I CAN'T WAIT UNTIL I TAKE MISS BELLE'S CLASS!
WHERE WERE YOU GUYS? YOU MISSED THE TIME TRAVEL POP QUIZ!
WE WERE JUST, UM--
--HELPING THE WALL WITH A SPECIAL ASSIGNMENT!
IVY, CAREFUL WITH THAT PLANT NOW. I BEST NOT SEE IT ON THE NEWS TOMORROW.
OF COURSE--
PRINCIPAL WALLER!

YOU'RE HERE!
HARLEY IS STILL WORKED UP FROM THE FIELD TRIP.
OH, YOUR TIME TRAVEL FIELD TRIP WAS TODAY THEN? I TRUST YOU GIRLS HAD A GOOD TIME.
IT WAS GREAT!
THE BESTEST TRIP I EVER DID FIELD! THANKS FOR LETTIN' US GO...
...AMANDA.
IT'S ME WHO SHOULD BE THANKING YOU.
...BUT IF YOU EVER CALL ME THAT AGAIN, YOU WILL GET DETENTION.
SOUNDS RIGHT TO ME!
YEP, IT'S ALL BACK TO NORMAL!
THE END!